MACPHERSON'S ISLAND

Grandpa has been ill and the nurse says he must have a holiday if he's to get better. Macpherson is very worried – they can't possibly afford a holiday and anyway, his miserly boss, Old Skinflint, would never let him leave the shop. But help comes unexpectedly from quiet Miss Peacock, and in no time at all she's actually persuaded Old Skinflint to drive Macpherson and Grandpa (and Maisie Murphy!) to Seagull Island to stay with her sister.

And what an adventurous holiday it turns out to be!

Cover illustration

ABOUT THE AUTHOR

Lavinia Derwent was born in No-Man's-Land on a farm on the Scottish side of the Border, so remote that she knew more animals than human-beings. Her head being full of 'beasts', she made up stories about them, invented a character called TAMMY TROOT and later an island called SULA, full of seals and sea-birds.

When she came to live in the big city of Glasgow she met many human-beings, but none that interested her more than a cheerful boy whom she saw in the street, lugging a heavy message-basket. MACPHERSON! Since then Macpherson has taken the place of 'beasts' in her head. Through him she has had many exciting adventures; and is delighted that so many children also follow his fortunes, sending her letters and drawings about Macpherson, Maisie and the other characters.

Lavinia Derwent has written many children's books. But of all her many characters she has the softest spot for MACPHERSON.

Macpherson's Island

Lavinia Derwent

Illustrated by Lesley Smith

KNIGHT BOOKS
Hodder and Stoughton

First published by Burke Publishing

This edition first published by Blackie & Son Limited in 1979

Knight Books edition 1980
Second impression 1981

The characters and situations in this book are entirely imaginary and bear no relation to any real person or actual happening

Reproduced, printed and bound in Great Britain for Hodder and Stoughton Paperbacks, a division of Hodder and Stoughton Ltd., Mill Road, Dunton Green, Sevenoaks, Kent (Editorial Office: 47 Bedford Square, London, WC1 3DP) by Cox & Wyman Ltd, Reading

ISBN 0 340 25498 X

Contents

1

The Adventure Begins

"This is the life," said Macpherson, lying back and gazing up at the sunny sky. "I feel just like Robinson Crusoe."

"Who'th he?" lisped the small girl by his side. Maisie Murphy was building a sand-castle, so lop-sided that it looked more like a Leaning Tower. She had gathered a heap of shells to decorate the door and the windows and the roof. It would be a fine castle if only it would stand up.

"Robinson Crusoe?" said Macpherson drowsily. "Och! He was a man in a book. He lived on an island like this."

But could there be another island as wonderful as this? The boy sat up to take a look around him. No, of course not! Nowhere else could there be a place so small yet so full of interest. Set in the middle of a Scottish loch, it had everything any boy could long for—a cave, an old castle, a sandy bay, a boat, a little jetty and, best of all, freedom.

It was only a dot on the map of Scotland,

yet it had a name of its own. Seagull Island they called it, and certainly there were plenty of sea-birds nesting on the rocks near by. Plenty of fish frisking in the water, too; and a family of swans who sailed across the loch like stately ships.

It was not a desert island, but there were few enough human beings living there: only Grandpa, sitting snoozing against an upturned boat, and Mr and Mrs Thing, pottering about in the castle garden.

Their real name was McConnochie, but it was too long and too difficult for Maisie. It was she who had christened them Mr and Mrs Thing, and neither of them seemed to mind.

"You can be calling us anything you like," said Mrs Thing, in her soft lilting voice. "Himself won't care."

Himself was her husband. He, in turn, referred to his wife as Herself; but Macpherson knew that her real name was Morag.

Morag McConnochie! He had first heard the name on a dull drizzly day in Glasgow, the day when the unexpected adventure started. At first it had been a bad day for Macpherson. To begin with, Grandpa was not at the window to wave goodbye from their new skyscraper flat. This, in itself, was enough to give a bad start to any day.

Macpherson liked living so high up in Clyde-View Tower. So did Grandpa. The old man was never tired of looking at the view over the city and beyond to the far-off hills. He loved seeing the boats on the winding River Clyde. It brought back memories of his old sailing days. Grandpa still felt connected with the sea, for all day long he sat at the window busily making ships-in-bottles.

Joey the budgie swung to and fro in his cage near by, imitating the old man's voice. "Ship ahoy! *Ho-ro, up she rises*! Hullo, Macpherson! Joey's a clever wee boy!"

The bird, too, seemed to enjoy being so high up. When he was let out of his cage, he fluttered at the window almost as if he was flying through the sky. Indeed, life in a skyscraper had opened up new worlds to them all, even Aunt Janet. She was forced to admit that the house was cleaner and easier to run than the old tenement flat where they used to live.

All the same, she still felt giddy when she gazed down from the high window. Nothing would persuade her to go up top, on to the roof of the Tower.

"Not if you offered me a fortune," she said,

setting her lips in a tight line. But who was likely to offer Aunt Janet a fortune? Certainly not Macpherson who was poorer than a church mouse.

"You're daft, you and your Grandpa," she scolded him one day when he and the old man decided to go up top for a blow. "A blow! You'll get blown away into the next kingdom, if you don't watch out. Or else you'll get your death of cold."

"Away, Janet woman!" said Grandpa, patting her on the arm as he went out of the door. "We'll get rid of our cobwebs. A good blow never did anyone any harm."

But for once he was wrong. Both he and Macpherson had caught severe chills. The boy was not worried about himself. He was young and strong. It was Grandpa who suffered most. The old man's chest was weak. He wheezed and coughed and grew thinner and paler.

The District Nurse came to visit him, and shook her head. "Away to your bed," she ordered him. "I don't like the look of you."

"No? And me thinking I was so handsome," said Grandpa, trying to make a joke, but it ended in a fit of coughing. Macpherson could tell from the way he gave in that Grandpa was feeling really ill.

"Are you very bad, Grandpa?" he asked anxiously, sitting by the bedside in the old man's narrow room.

"Bad? No, not me! I'm always good!" There was still a twinkle in Grandpa's eyes; but it was an effort for him to speak, even to Macpherson. "Away you go; I'm needing my beauty-sleep."

Macpherson's heart sank when he went through to the living-room and heard what the District Nurse was saying to Aunt Janet. "No! I don't like the look of him. He's getting on, you know. You can't expect much at his age."

The boy knew, of course, that Grandpa was old; but he was still so young at heart that age did not seem to matter. All the same, he was growing thinner and frailer every day.

"A chill at his age isn't so easy to throw off," went on the District Nurse. "He needs building up, poor old thing."

Macpherson had never thought of Grandpa as a poor old thing. As the boy trudged the city streets that day he puzzled over the problem—how to build Grandpa up. The streets seemed drearier than ever. The message-basket was heavier. Mr McGlashan, the grocer, was meaner, more like his nickname—Old Skinflint—than his real name. The only one who never changed was Miss Peacock, the shop-assistant. She was as kind and pleasant as ever.

When Macpherson pushed open the shop-door he heard her talking to Old Skinflint.

"Morag McConnochie! That's the answer."

"What?" It was the wrong answer for Old Skinflint who was busy totting up the books. This was the most important job of the day, to find out how much money he had made. He looked at her over his spectacles and said sharply, "What's all this about, Miss Peacock? You know I don't like being interrupted ..."

"I know, Mr McGlashan," she said, interrupting him again. Macpherson was surprised at her. It was not like Miss Peacock to be so bold. "I was thinking of Morag McConnochie."

"Who in the world is she?" asked the grocer impatiently.

"My cousin."

"You and your cousins! You have them all over the world. You'll likely have one on the moon, too." He shot her a sharp glance. "Have you cleared up the back-shop?"

"No, I haven't," said Misss Peacock. "I mean, I have cleared out the back-shop but I haven't got a cousin on the moon. I've got one on Seagull Island: Morag McConnochie. She comes from Skye."

"Well, that's near enough the moon," said Old Skinflint, with an unusual touch of humour. All the same, he was not amused. "What are you gaping at?" he asked sharply, when he saw Macpherson staring at him.

"Nothing," said Macpherson, moving towards the safety of the back-shop.

"Wait," said Miss Peacock, catching him by the arm. "It's you I was thinking about,

Macpherson. You and your Grandpa. You'd both be the better for a holiday on the island. My cousin takes in boarders. You could go there for a fortnight. You'd like a holiday on Seagull Island, wouldn't you, Macpherson?"

Macpherson stared at her, wondering if she had gone mad. Fancy making such a daft suggestion in front of Old Skinflint who hated the very word holiday. Hard work was all he thought about. Holidays were a waste of time. Had Miss Peacock something up her sleeve?

The grocer glared at her under his bushy eyebrows. "Stop talking nonsense," he said crossly. "What's the use of putting such silly ideas into the boy's head? There's enough rubbish there already. As for your cousins, Miss Peacock, the less I hear about them the better. You can keep them to yourself."

"Very well, Mr McGlashan," said Miss Peacock mildly, but with a gleam in her eye. Macpherson was certain-sure she was up to something. "I'll keep them to myself. Especially Robert Reid, my cousin from America. He made his fortune out there...."

"What?" The word *fortune* was more to Old Skinflint's liking than the word *holiday*. He looked eagerly at Miss Peacock and asked, "Is he very rich, this cousin of yours?"

"So they say," she replied. "But he's still keen on business. In fact, he's coming back to Glasgow to start a chain of restaurants." She gave the grocer a sidelong look. "He would be a good customer for the shop, wouldn't he? Think what a lot of groceries he'd need. I could get him to come here." Miss Peacock turned away and gave a little wink to Macpherson. "But, of course, you don't want to hear about my cousins, Mr McGlashan. . . ."

"Oh, yes, I do!" Old Skinflint almost jumped over the counter to reach Miss Peacock's side. He grasped her by the arm and cried, "I'd be most grateful. Most grateful, indeed! A chain of restaurants! We could get splendid orders. Splendid!" He licked his lips at the very thought of them. "You wouldn't let your cousin pass my door, would you, Miss Peacock?"

Miss Peacock gave him a cool look. She had the upper hand for once. "No, I wouldn't, Mr McGlashan," she said brightly. "So it's all settled. You'll let Macpherson off for a fortnight."

"What? What's that you're saying?" His bushy eyebrows shot up and down. "We're not talking about Macpherson. We're talking about your cousin."

"That's right! My cousin, Morag McConnochie. Macpherson and his Grandpa are going to stay with her on the island. And what's more," she added in a determined voice, "you're going to drive them up there. Meantime, I'll contact my cousin Robert. Unless, of course you don't want to meet him."

It was blackmail, of course! Old Skinflint spluttered and gasped like a hooked fish, but there was nothing else for it but to accept Miss

Peacock's terms.

"All right," he said gruffly. "I'll do as you say."

"I thought you would," she said calmly, and followed Macpherson into the back-shop.

"Oh, Miss Peacock, you're a corker!" cried the boy, clutching her by the waist and whirling her round in a wild dance. "I never knew you had it in you."

"Oh, I'm not as soft as I look," said Miss Peacock with a flush of victory on her cheeks. "You've got to play Old Skinflint at his own game."

Macpherson suddenly looked serious. "You haven't made up your cousin, Miss Peacock?" he asked her. "The one from America?"

"Oh no; he's real enough. I'll stick to my side of the bargain," promised Miss Peacock. "But never mind my cousin Robert. It's my cousin Morag you'll be meeting soon. You'll like living on an island, Macpherson?"

"Like it!" he said, turning a somersault among the crates of tinned soup. "Not half!"

So that was why, a few days later, he and Grandpa were sitting in the back of Old Skinflint's car. It was a plain, no-nonsense motor-car, sadly in need of some new paint;

and the grocer was an angry driver.

"Silly goat!" he shouted at a cyclist. "D'you want to be killed? Crazy fool! There's nothing but idiots on the roads nowadays."

The small girl sitting beside him bounced up and down and began to ask tactless questions.

"I thay! Why do they call you Old Thkinflint?"

Macpherson held his breath. Maisie Murphy! She had no right to be there, anyway, and certainly no right to be asking questions like that. What on earth would the grocer say?

"Silly goat!" He was shouting at a motor-cyclist this time. Then he shot a quick look at Maisie and said, "What was that? Speak up!"

Macpherson hastily leant forward and tapped her on the shoulder. "Treacle toffee!" he hissed at her.

At the magic words Maisie whipped round. "Where?" she asked greedily.

"Here," said Macpherson, rustling a paper bag. "Aunt Janet made it for me to take to Mrs McConnochie."

"Oh!" Maisie twisted her neck as far as it would go and looked longingly at the paper bag. "Ith Mithith—er—Thing to get it all?"

"You might get a piece if you promise to keep quiet," bribed Macpherson.

"Oh yeth, I will!" Maisie beamed with delight. "A big bit, pleathe!" But even a big bit could not stop Maisie's tongue. It was no trouble to her to suck and speak at the same time.

Macpherson scowled at her back view and wished she had been left behind. Not that she had been invited. She had just got into the front seat and refused to budge. "I'm coming, too," she announced, and that was that.

It was Macpherson who had to run back

and tell the Murphies. One more or one less in their topsy-turvy household made little difference. All the same, he felt it his duty.

"Maisie's coming with us," he said breathlessly. "Is that okay? Nothing'll stop her."

"Sure! Bedad, away and enjoy yourselves, Macpherson me boyo, and the best of luck to yez all," said Murphy cheerfully. "I'd come meself if I had the chance."

As for clothes, Maisie just went as she was. Any cast-off garment was good enough for her. Today she wore a striped football-jersey and an old skirt of her mother's; much too long and too wide. It was fastened round her waist with a large safety-pin, in great danger of coming adrift every time she moved. Not that Maisie minded. She was away on her holidays.

"Ithn't it great?" she said blissfully, sucking at her toffee and bouncing up and down in her seat.

"Sit still and keep quiet," said Old Skinflint crossly.

"Yeth! Okay!" said Maisie happily; but nobody, not even the grim-faced grocer, could stop her chatter. She talked to him non-stop in the same tone she used to the Murphy babies, and even began to sing *Diddle-diddle-dumpling, my son John.*

Macpherson's face grew redder when she turned to the driver and asked, "Do you never thmile? Ith that why they call you Old Thkinflint?"

A stray lamb wandering across the road diverted the driver's attention, and the question was never answered. "Silly goat!" he shouted at the surprised animal. "Watch where you're going."

"It'th not a goat; it'th a lamb," Maisie corrected him; but the grocer paid no attention. Everything he met was a silly goat, even the branch of a tree which had been blown across the road.

Grandpa sat up and sniffed the clean fresh air. He had been half asleep beside Macpherson, but now he began to look more alive. "Ship ahoy!" he said, taking a deep breath. "That smells good. Look, Macpherson, there's the Ben."

The Ben was a high mountain with white clouds drifting across its topmost peak. It could be seen, not only where it stood, but also reflected in the waters of the loch near by. And there, in the middle of the loch, was the island.

"That's it!" cried Macpherson. "We're here!"

"Thank goodness!" grunted Old Skinflint.

"Get out everybody, and let me turn the car. Goodness knows how many more silly goats I'll meet on the way home to Glasgow."

2

Seagull Island

Morag McConnochie's husband—soon to be known as Mr Thing—was waiting for them with the motorboat. He had one other passenger, the largest and ugliest dog they had ever seen.

"Hullo, you!" said Maisie, patting the dog's shaggy coat. "What'th your name?"

The dog turned his back on her, so it was left to Mr Thing to reply. "He hasn't got a name," he said, helping Maisie on board. "We just call him the dog! He's plain, but he has a nice nature."

Mr Thing, too, had a nice nature, though he was not so plain. His weather-beaten face crinkled up when he smiled, and his eyes were deep blue and full of fun. He wore a navy-blue jersey and long waders up to his thighs; and he had an air about him of being ready to cope with any kind of wind and weather. But what Macpherson liked best about him was the kindly way he looked after Grandpa, without making him feel too old and feeble.

"Sit here, Captain," he said, helping Grandpa to the best seat, already occupied by the plain dog. "Move over, dog! We've got a real sea-dog in the boat today; isn't that right, Captain?" Grandpa looked pleased at the compliment. When he was settled, Mr Thing started up the engine. Away went the little boat puttering across the loch.

Macpherson and Maisie sat side by side trying to look at everything at once, first on one side and then on the other. "You'll be feeling peckish," said Mr Thing, steering for the little island. "We'll be there in two or three minutes, and Herself will have the supper ready."

"Who'th Herthelf?" asked Maisie, letting the dog nibble at her fingers.

"The missis! She's not a bad cook. Look! There's the castle."

Seagull Castle! It was the only building on the island, a story-book castle with turrets and towers and grey stone walls. It seemed to be sailing towards them, though Macpherson knew, of course, it was the other way round.

"Jings!" he cried in delight. "Are we going to live there? It's like Buckingham Palace!"

Macpherson had never seen Buckingham Palace except in his imagination, but this was real enough. He could see the seagulls circling round the tower and resting on the turrets. There was a flagpole right at the top. Maybe he could climb up there and raise his own standard—the lion rampant. Then everyone would know that Macpherson the Brave, King of Scotland, was in residence.

Maisie took one look at the castle and said, "It'th not ath high ath our thkythraper. Which floor do you live on, Mr Thing?"

"Och, I don't live on the floor," said Mr Thing, wrinkling up his face into a smile. "There are plenty of rooms. The missis and I have the run of the whole place. Caretakers, you might say, keeping the castle high and dry for his lordship. Lord Kyle, that is. Not that he lives here nowadays. It's more or less a ruin. Heave ho! We're here!"

The dog was the first to leap on shore and stood watching every move as Grandpa was helped out of the boat. Grandpa was looking shaky as he stumbled across the shingly beach; but Macpherson was there to steady him and Mr Thing called cheerfully, "We'll all be feeling in better shape once we've had some food.'"

It was a great meal! Herself must have been baking for hours. There were pancakes and

gingerbread and scones and oatcakes and fruit tarts. There was home-made jam and real butter, and there were two boiled eggs each.

"Two!" Maisie's eyes goggled when Mrs Thing placed the eggs on her plate and put a little woolly cover over one of them to keep it warm. At home Maisie was lucky if she got the top of one egg. "Oh my! Thith ith great!"

Mrs Thing looked rather like an egg herself, a brown egg, all smooth and plump and shiny. Her hair was brown and so were her eyes. Even her face was tanned by the sun and the wind, except for a rosy flush on her cheeks.

She sat at the top of the table, pouring out the tea from a fat tea-pot. The cups were so big that Maisie had to use both hands to lift hers.

"Eat up," cried Mrs Thing, beaming at them and passing plates in all directions. "You're a peaky-looking lot, but I'll soon be putting some flesh on you."

Macpherson smiled at her as he knocked the top off his second egg. Mrs Thing spoke as if she was fattening them up for the market. He took an anxious look at Grandpa. The old man was toying with his food and coughing between each bite. The boy's heart sank when he saw how thin and pale Grandpa looked. It would be a long time before *he* was ready for the market.

They were eating in the kitchen with its stone-flagged floor and open fireplace where great logs of wood blazed and crackled. Macpherson longed to explore the rest of the castle and find out where they were going to sleep. The nearer the top the better.

Mrs Thing seemed to guess his thoughts. "There are two little rooms in the tower for you and Maisie," she told him. "Your Grandpa had better sleep downstairs. It'll save him that it was the donkey who was master. The boy tried being firm. "Come along now; stop your nonsense, you stupid thing!" He tried coaxing. "Good wee donkey; stand still, like a clever beast!"

No use. Dum-Dum let Macpherson slither halfway on to his back, then kicked up his heels and shook the boy off. "*Haw-haw-haw!*"

"I think he'th having a good laugh at uth," said Maisie, helping Macpherson up for the third time.

"He's a silly thing," said the boy sulkily. "I don't care. Let him go."

Mr Thing came out of the castle garden carrying a large basket of vegetables. "Hi! Dum-Dum! Carrot!" he called to the donkey who let out a loud "*Haw-haw*" and came prancing forward to receive his daily treat. "Would you like a ride, Macpherson?" asked Mr Thing. "Wait; I'll lift you up."

It was a fine feeling ambling along on the donkey's back. Not that Macpherson had any say as to where they should go. He just went where Dum-Dum took him. The donkey stopped and started as he pleased and looked round now and then to see if Maisie and the dog were following.

"Can I have a turn, Macpherthon?" Maisie

kept asking.

"Not yet."

"Okay; I'll jutht walk," said Maisie, used to making sacrifices.

Macpherson was now in one of his show-off moods. "Watch me," he called to Maisie. "No hands!"

He thrust his hands into his pockets and swayed about on the donkey's back. All went well till Dum-Dum suddenly swerved round a corner. Down fell the warrior in the dust, and that was that.

"Silly thing! I've had enough of you," said Macpherson, chasing the donkey away. "Come along, Maisie; we'll explore on our feet."

All the same, Dum-Dum had no intention of being left behind. He and the dog followed Macpherson and Maisie wherever they went. They jumped across streams, scrambled up hillocks, and thrust their way through the shrubs and trees of a little wood in the middle of the island. All roads, of course, led back to the shore.

The donkey stood in the water to cool his legs, while the dog stretched out on the shingle beside Grandpa.

"Well?" said the old man, opening one eye.

said happily. "I'm sure he never eats a decent bite of food when he's away from home. I like to fatten him up at the weekends."

She was great for fattening people up, was Mrs Thing. Already Macpherson could see a difference in Grandpa. His cheeks were less sunken, his face had more colour in it, and his step was brisker. His cough had almost vanished. "Heave ho, my hearty! I'll reach my century yet!" he told Macpherson.

"Oh, I hope so, Grandpa!" Macpherson settled the old man in his favourite spot, with his back against a rock, and sprawled on the sand waiting for the Boy to come. Mr Thing had gone across in the boat to fetch him, with the dog on board. They would be back, according to Mr Thing, in two toots.

"Are the two tootth not up yet?" asked Maisie. The sand-castle she had built had come tumbling down like one of the old Glasgow tenements. She was wondering whether to start another or get ready to welcome the boy.

"They're coming," cried Macpherson, jumping up. He could see the boat leaving the pier across the water, and strained his eyes for a first glimpse of his future playmate. He could see two figures on board—Mr Thing with a tall man beside him. But where was the Boy?

As they came nearer Mr Thing waved and shouted, "Ahoy! Here we come!" He steered the boat towards the little jetty, and Macpherson ran to meet him, calling out, "Where's the Boy?"

"He's here," beamed Mr Thing, pointing to his tall companion.

Macpherson gaped, and all his hopes of finding a playmate faded when he saw that the Boy was a grown man.

3

The Ben

"Smile, please!"

Roderick McAlpine McConnochie, otherwise known as the Boy, was taking a photograph. They were all in it, even the dog and Dum-Dum. Indeed, the donkey seemed to be smiling more broadly than any of them.

"Wait till I tidy my hair," cried Maisie, trying to smooth down her tousled curls. "How do I look, Macpherthon?"

"Same as ever," said Macpherson, not bothering to glance at her.

But it was not true. Maisie was looking a treat! She was wearing a new frock; or, at least, one made out of an old summer dress of Mrs Thing's. It had pink flowers all over it, the same colour as in Maisie's cheeks.

Mrs Thing's sewing-machine had been whirring away merrily. Another dress—blue this time—was in the process of being made. "Take off that football-jersey," she told Maisie. "It makes you look like a bumble-bee."

Maisie looked more like a butterfly today as

she smiled sweetly at the Boy's camera. It was difficult to think of him as the Boy, but at least he was still young at heart, even though he was so tall, and a teacher.

"A *teacher!*" Macpherson had cried, looking up at him in dismay. Teachers, in Macpherson's opinion, were not human. But this one was different. For one thing, he had a sense of humour. The Boy was outsize in every way. He shouted rather than talked. He roared with laughter. He ate twice as much as anyone else; and when he walked, he set such a pace that few could keep up with him. Little wonder that Seagull Island was too small for the Boy. Yet he seemed happy enough to be home.

"That's it!" he said, clicking the camera. "I've got you all in. A fine lot of beauties you are, too! I'll see that you get a copy."

Maisie ran forward to look at the camera. "Can I thee mythelf now?" she asked eagerly.

"No, you'll have to wait. I'll post it to you. What's your address?"

"Glathgow."

"It's Clyde-View Tower, Glasgow," said Macpherson, coming to the rescue.

"A skyscraper, eh? Is it very high?" asked the Boy.

"Yeth," said Maisie, looking up at him.

"About ath high ath—ath you."

The Boy threw back his head and laughed. Meantime, Macpherson was puzzling over a problem. What should he call the tall man? He could hardly keep on calling him the Boy.

"Mr—er—McConnochie," he began; "what shall I call you?"

"Anything you like." The Boy gave him a broad grin. "The children at school call me Mr Mac. In front of my face, that is! My name's Roderick. Why not call me that?"

"Okay," said Macpherson, greatly relieved; and having solved one problem he now brought up the subject nearest to his heart. The Ben!

"Roderick, would you take me up the Ben?" he asked his new friend. "I'd love to climb it. Mr Thing—er—your father—said you might take me."

"Of course," boomed Roderick. "Any time you like. I always enjoy a wee walk up the Ben."

A wee walk! Roderick, like his father, spoke of the Ben as if it were nothing more than a hillock. A few steps and he would be at the top! Macpherson wondered how *he* would be able to keep up with him, but he was determined to do his best.

"When can we start?" he asked eagerly.

"Tomorrow morning," said Roderick. "Bright and early."

Macpherson slept little that night, not being sure when bright and early was. At dawn he looked out of the window of his tower bedroom. Not a sight of the Ben! "Mercy me! Has it vanished?" thought the boy in a panic. What if it was not a real mountain? Perhaps it came and went, like a ghost.

Like a ghost, it gradually appeared through the morning mist and Macpherson's doubts were gone. It was real enough and before the day was out Macpherson the Explorer would reach the top. Maybe he would plant a little flag there in honour of the great occasion, a flag with the Scottish lion on it.

He dressed quickly and went downstairs. He crept along the winding passages, not knowing if anyone else was up. As he drew nearer the kitchen he sniffed the appetising smell of bacon. Someone else was up bright and early.

Mrs Thing rose from the table. "Come along, Macpherson," she said, setting a place for him. "You're just in time. The Boy's at his breakfast."

What a breakfast! Mr and Mrs Thing looked on proudly as their son made short work of the platefuls set before him. He had already polished off a large bowl of porridge and was now enjoying his bacon and eggs.

"Tuck in, Boy," his mother said, pouring tea into an outsize cup. "You've got to keep up your strength. Sit down, Macpherson, and I'll serve your porridge."

Macpherson's appetite was good, but it was nothing like the Boy's. He had finished and was sitting back, full to the brim, while the big man was still eating.

"That's right, Boy. Another piece of toast," said Mr Thing, pushing the butter and marmalade nearer to his son. "Eat your fill!"

The dog sat watching him, and Dum-Dum wandered in, looking for his morning titbit. Meantime, Mrs Thing was busy packing up food for their trip, enough to keep an expedition going. One thing was certain, they were not likely to starve. She packed a large haversack for her son and a smaller one for Macpherson. "In case you fancy a wee bite on the way. It'll keep your strength up. Are you sure you've had enough, Boy?"

"Yes, thanks, Mum. Enough to keep me going." He patted his well-filled stomach. "All the same, I'll be ready for supper when I get back. What's it to be?"

"Steak-and-kidney," his mother told him; "with apple-dumpling to follow."

"Apple-dumpling, eh?" Roderick McAlpine McConnochie smacked his lips. "Come on, Macpherson; let's work up an appetite." He swung his haversack over his shoulder. "Are you ready?"

"Ay, ay, sir!" Macpherson was eager to be off before Maisie came on the scene. She would be sure to want to join them. He had told Grandpa, of course, but Maisie had been kept in the dark. It would spoil everything to have a small girl trailing behind them up the Ben.

Dum-Dum and the dog followed them down to the boat. The dog jumped on board. No question of leaving him behind! "Och! he knows his way up the Ben blindfold," said Roderick, patting the animal's rough coat. "We're away, Macpherson!"

Just then a small barefoot figure appeared with one of Mrs Thing's nightgowns tucked around her. She waved and called, "Macpher-thon! Where are you going?"

"Nowhere," said Macpherson crossly.

"Can I come with you?"

"No."

"Why not?" begged Maisie, coming so near the water that her nightgown trailed into it.

"Because!" said Macpherson with a final note in his voice.

Even from a distance he could see Maisie's lip begin to tremble and the tears roll down her cheeks. She was a great one for turning on the waterworks, was Maisie. But Macpherson was determined to harden his heart.

"What about it?" asked Roderick, willing to turn back. "Will we let the lassie come?"

"No! She'd just be a nuisance."

"Maybe you're right." Roderick poked about in his haversack and found a rosy-red apple. "Here!" he called, tossing it with a mighty throw across the water. "A wee present!"

The apple landed high and dry on the beach. Maisie picked it up and called, "Thankth!" But her cheeks were still wet with tears. All day long Macpherson remembered that last view of her, as she stood beside Dum-Dum, sharing her apple with him.

The boat reached the other side of the loch in no time, or in what Mr Thing would have called two toots. But it took many more toots before they reached the foot of the Ben. "Jings! It seems to move further away every time I look at it," said Macpherson, eager to begin his climb. "D'you think we'll ever reach it?"

"Of course! Step out, Macpherson!"

They had to trudge a long way along the road. Then they climbed over a fence, crossed a field, walked up a winding pathway—and there they were at last, at the foot of the mountain.

Macpherson was used to long treks in the Glasgow streets. He stepped out briskly, but even so it was difficult to keep up with the Boy's strides. Roderick roared out a song as he tramped along. "*Step we gaily as we go, heel for heel and toe for toe.*"

The sun rose high in the sky. Macpherson's haversack grew heavier, and his feet began to drag. "Let's have a breather before we start climbing," suggested Roderick, more for Macpherson's sake than his own.

The dog lay down on the grass, panting heavily. Macpherson joined him, while Roderick opened out his haversack in search of food. "We'd better have a bite to keep us going," he said, unearthing some hefty-looking sandwiches. "I'm feeling a bit peckish."

Macpherson was surprised to find that he, too, was hungry in spite of his enormous breakfast. He ate a ham sandwich and an apple, and began to feel better. He could easily climb to the top; no trouble at all!

He was the first on his feet. "Come on, Roderick; we're wasting time."

"Not so fast, youngster! Don't rush at it like a bull at a gate," said the large man, calmly. "Slow and steady does it."

It was easy enough on the lower slopes. Only a wee walk! The grass was soft and springy, with tiny wild flowers growing here and there. Birds twittered overhead, flying upwards as if they, too, were climbing the Ben.

"That's a skylark," said Roderick, imitating its tune. "Listen! And that's a curlew." He knew them all, and could twitter their call. In between, he shouted out his songs: *Speed, bonnie boat, like a bird on the wing; On the bonnie bonnie banks of Loch Lomond;* and *What shall we do with the drunken sailor?*

Now and then they paused to look back at Seagull Island. The higher they climbed the smaller it looked, till it seemed only a tiny dot set in the sparkling waters of the loch. They could see the outline of the castle, but no human beings. Macpherson wondered what Grandpa was doing and if Maisie's tears were dry by now.

The mountain grew steeper, and now the real climb began. The dog led the way, as sure-footed as a goat. Roderick followed, shouting back to Macpherson, "Watch your step, youngster. If you tumble you'll roll right to the bottom. *Ha-ha-ha! You and me. Little brown jug, don't I love thee!*"

Macpherson wondered where he got enough breath to climb and sing at the same time. He himself was soon puffing and panting. He had to heave himself up, clutching for support at clumps of heather and bracken. The air felt keener and fresher the higher they went.

"Goodness gracious!" gasped Macpherson as he came across a white patch in a sheltered spot. "It's snow! In the middle of summer!"

"Och ay!" said Roderick, turning to look. "It's left there by Jack Frost so that the Snow Man'll know where to come next winter! *Crying cockles and mussels alive, alive O!*"

Macpherson was glad it was not winter right now, though he could imagine how beautiful the Ben would look when covered with an icing of snow. He was glad, too, when Roderick called a halt for another breather.

"I'm feeling peckish again," he boomed, swinging the haversack from his shoulder; but it was for Macpherson's sake that he stopped. He could see that the "wee walk" was hard going for the boy.

Macpherson sat down thankfully and gazed at the faraway island, feeling that it was all a dream. If he half-closed his eyes he could see it fading away, castle and all. Perhaps he would wake up and find himself in the Glasgow skyscraper instead of the topmost peak of the Ben.

Roderick sat up, breaking the spell, and asking, "What's that?" Something seemed to be buzzing over their heads, like a giant bee.

"It's a helicopter," cried Macpherson, wide

LSJS.

awake now. This was no dream. The helicopter was real enough, hovering overhead as if looking for somewhere to land. "I wonder where it's going?"

"I know!" cried Roderick. "Wait and see! It's going to land on Seagull Island."

"Fancy that!" gasped Macpherson. "So it is!" He watched the helicopter flying over the loch, then hovering over the little island, ready for landing.

"It's Lord Kyle," explained Roderick. "He often drops in. It's a pity you're missing him, Macpherson. He might have taken you up for a flip."

"Oh!" Macpherson looked down in the mouth for a moment at the thought of what he had missed. Lucky Maisie! Maybe she would get a flip instead. "Och well! I can't have everything," he consoled himself. After all, it was better to conquer the Ben on his own feet rather than let someone fly him around in a machine. All the same, he strained his eyes for another sight of the helicopter but it had disappeared from view behind the castle.

"Come along, youngster!" called Roderick, heaving himself up. "Brace yourself for the last lap. *Ha-ha-ha! You and me . .*"

Macpherson braced himself. He was determined to get to the top even if he had to crawl on his hands and knees; and, indeed, as the Ben grew steeper, it seemed easier to creep than to climb up the final peak. He did not pause to look back. It took all his energy to pull himself up, one step at a time. His arms were aching; his knees were bruised; his heart was thumping, but he kept going. He would make it! Macpherson the Brave would reach the top!

Roderick had already made it. He was standing like a giant on top of the world. "Hi, Macpherson!" he called in a triumphant voice, "I'm here! Hurry up! It's great! Wait till you see the view!"

There were more patches of slippery snow near the top. Macpherson stood up, ready to make his final spurt. He would boast about this to Maisie. Wait till he told Miss Peacock. "Och yes, I got to the top of the Ben. It was just a wee walk!"

He had only a few more steps to go when his foot slipped in the snow. Roderick shouted a warning. "Look out!" Too late; the boy had already lost his balance.

It was easier going down than coming up! Macpherson rolled over and over like a barrel, gathering speed as he made his rapid descent.

He could see the sky and snow and the heather all turning somersaults with him. He tried frantically to clutch at a patch of bracken as he hurtled past, but he just could not stop.

Macpherson felt as if he had rolled for ages. Indeed, he was more than halfway down before he jolted to a halt against a small sturdy tree. He lay there panting, bruised and battered all over, like a damaged apple. Tears began to well up in his eyes. Macpherson the Conqueror had come a cropper!

Gradually, he pulled himself together and picked himself up. No bones broken! "It could have been worse," he told himself. "I can still walk. One-two-three! And up I go again!"

He had just started his second climb when Roderick came careering down the hillside, with a look of concern on his face. "Are you all in one piece, Macpherson?"

"Yes, yes! I'm fine!"

Roderick skidded to a standstill. "Fine? Well, you've certainly had a fine tumble. Never saw anyone go down the Ben faster! Sit down, youngster, and take a breather. Where's your haversack?"

"Lost!" said Macpherson; but what did it matter? All he wanted was to start again and get to the top. He struggled to his feet, but

Roderick held him back.

"Don't be silly, youngster! You can't go now. Look at the mist."

Macpherson stared upwards and gave a start of surprise when he saw that the top of the Ben was hidden under a white misty cloud. It came swirling down the mountain-side to meet them. Another moment and they, too, would be lost.

"Hurry, Macpherson! Let's get down as fast as we can," said Roderick, with a note of urgency in his voice.

Just then the dog began to howl. It was an eerie, uneasy sound, as if he sensed that something was wrong. "Listen!" cried Macpherson; "he's heard something."

True enough, though the mist there came a call for help, faint and far away.

4

To The Rescue

"It often happens like this on the Ben. The mist appears from nowhere, all of a sudden. It's a blessing we're far enough down," said Roderick, keeping a close grip of Macpherson's arm. "Which direction would you say the shout came from?"

"Goodness knows," said Macpherson in a puzzled voice. It was anybody's guess. The cry for help had stopped; and now they seemed to be playing Blind Man's Buff in a maze of white woolly fog.

"We'd better try shouting," decided Roderick—and when Roderick shouted it was a sound no one was likely to miss! "*HUL-LOO-OO IS THERE ANYONE THERE?*"

Only an echo came back to them through the mist. Then the dog suddenly bounded forward and gave an excited bark. "He's found something!" cried Roderick. "Let's follow him, Macpherson."

The dog led them to a rocky hollow where a figure lay, huddled and helpless. It was the last person Macpherson expected to see. "Goodness gracious me!" he gasped. "It's Old Skinflint!"

"Old Who?" asked Roderick, bending down to look.

"Mr McGlashan, the grocer," said Macpherson in a dazed voice. "What in the world is he doing here?"

Old Skinflint lying unconscious on the Ben! Surely this must be a dream! The mist, the echoing voices, the faraway feeling, made everything seem remote and unreal. In another moment he would wake up in his skyscraper bedroom with Aunt Janet calling, "Get up, Macpherson, and look slippy!"

A moan came from the huddled figure. He was real enough! Macpherson knelt down and peered at him through the mist. Who else but Old Skinflint could have such bushy eyebrows and such an angry expression even when he was only half-conscious?

"He's coming round. It's his ankle, I think. He must have slipped and given it a sudden twist," said Roderick, as he tried to raise him up into a more comfortable position. "That's better! How are you feeling now, sir?"

The eyebrows shot up and down as Old Skinflint glared at his rescuers. When he saw Macpherson his expression became even angrier. "What on earth are you doing here?" he said crossly, as if it was all the boy's fault.

Macpherson might have asked the same question. Instead, he bent over him and said meekly, "I'm on my holidays. Don't you remember, Mr Skin—er—Mr McGlashan, sir? Are you all right?"

"Of course, I'm all right," snapped the grocer, trying to raise himself up. "Stupid idiot!" he groaned, as he felt the stinging pain in his ankle; but whether he was referring to himself, Macpherson, or the ankle, it was impossible to tell.

"What'll we do?" asked the boy, looking at Roderick for guidance.

"Do? Och, we'll help him down, and I'll get Dr Brown at the village to patch him up. You take one side, Macpherson, and I'll take the other. Easy does it!"

They heaved Old Skinflint on to one foot and half hauled, half carried him down the Ben. He was no light burden; nor did he do much to help himself, apart from groaning, "Silly idiot! Never again!"

His anger, it appeared, was directed against himself. And against Macpherson, too; for, in a way, it was all the boy's fault. If he—Mr McGlashan—had not been forced to drive the

message-boy to his holiday island, he would never have thought about the Ben. But he *had* thought about it; and on a sudden impulse had decided to come back and climb it.

"What on earth got into me, goodness knows," groaned the grocer, hopping down the mountain-side. "Stupid goat! I should have more sense." He glared at Macpherson. "And so should you! Wasting your time gallivanting about on a mountain. Wait till I get you back to the shop. Message-boys! They're all idiots!"

Macpherson never forgot that journey down the Ben, with the cobwebby mist swirling around them, and Old Skinflint grunting and groaning at each step. The dog led the way, turning round now and again to see if they were following. Then suddenly the mist began to clear. They could hear the faint call of a cuckoo, and next moment they emerged into bright sunshine near the foot of the mountain.

"That's the Ben for you!" said Roderick cheerfully. "It takes turns! Thank goodness, it's taking a turn for the better now. Cheer up, sir! We'll have you at the doctor's in two toots."

"I don't want any doctor," growled Old Skinflint. "I can't stand them; they're all silly fools. What I want is to get into my car and drive home to Glasgow."

"I doubt if you'll be able to drive with your ankle in that state. I tell you what," said Roderick, in a reasoning voice; "why not come over with us to the island and lie up for a day or two? It would do you a world of good."

Old Skinflint looked at him as if he were mad. "Don't talk rubbish," he said in a sharp voice. "I've got my shop to run." He turned his anger on Macpherson. "It's all very well for the likes of you to take time off. A fat lot you care whether I go bankrupt or not."

He was whipping himself up into one of his furies, angered by pain and the fact that he had to be half carried like a baby. It was enough to try the patience of a saint, and the grocer was never in a saintly mood at the best of times. But before they reached the village it was obvious, even to Old Skinflint, that something must be done about his ankle.

"All right, then; I'll see the stupid doctor, but I won't promise to do what he tells me."

Dr Brown looked at the ankle, strapped a bandage round it and said, "There! You'll be all right. No bones broken, but I advise you to put your feet up for a few days."

Macpherson waited for the outburst, but none came. Old Skinflint limped out, leaning on Roderick's arm, without even muttering that the doctor was a silly goat. His face looked white and strained; and when Roderick steered him towards the boat lying at the jetty, he made no protest.

Macpherson could scarcely believe it as they sailed across the loch. If anyone had told him they would be bringing Old Skinflint back to the Island, he would have laughed at such a ridiculous idea. It was a strange world, right enough, as strange as a dream. Anything could happen, even when you were wide awake.

Macpherson looked back at the Ben. Not a sign of mist! He could see right to the top, to the spot which he had failed to reach. His bruises were beginning to hurt. In the excitement of rescuing Old Skinflint, he had forgotten about them; but now he began to feel sorry for himself. Especially when he heard a whirr in the air and saw the giant bumble-bee take off.

"That's Lord Kyle away in his helicopter," boomed Roderick, steering for the little landing-stage. "He'll likely have waited till the mist cleared. It's a pity you missed him, Macpherson."

"Huh!" said Macpherson. This was not his lucky day; but soon the sulky look left his face. Grandpa, looking fit and sunburnt, was waiting on the shore to welcome him.

"Ship ahoy, Macpherson, my boy! It's great to see you back!"

The old man looked so full of vigour that Macpherson's small troubles vanished. What did getting to the top of the Ben matter, or having a ride in a helicopter? As long as Grandpa was well, everything was okay.

"Eat up, Mr McGlashan!" cried Mrs Thing, stretching her hand out for the grocer's plate. "Some more potatoes? Another helping of steak-and-kidney? A little gravy? Pass in your plate. Deary me! I never saw anyone with such a poor appetite."

Old Skinflint had never seen anyone with such big appetites! Across the table sat Roderick wolfing his second helping, or maybe it was his third. As for the helpings, they would have lasted the grocer a week.

The very thought of such a lavish way of living horrified him. His bushy brows shot up and down when he saw the dog and the donkey being fed with rich titbits. The jugs of cream, the cakes, tarts, scones, butter, and jam were all too much for him, not to mention the carefree chatter round the table. "Waste not want not" was his motto, and it applied to words as well as food.

The only silent member of the company was Macpherson. He was eating little and saying less. It was not only because his bruises were hurting. The truth was that he did not feel at ease sitting at the same table as the grocer. Every moment he expected Old Skinflint to shout, "Macpherson! Where's that lazy message-boy? Have you delivered all the groceries? Did you take care not to shoogle the eggs? Go and sweep out the back-shop. Stir your stumps, or I'll flay you alive! Message-boys! They're all silly goats!"

How could Macpherson enjoy his steak-and-kidney pudding with those piercing eyes watching every bite? The others did not seem to mind. They seemed to be taking Old Skinflint in their stride.

"D'you know what, Macpherthon?" said Maisie, with a forkful of potatoes halfway to her mouth. "I've theen a helicopter."

"So have I," snapped Macpherson.

"Oh!" Maisie looked like a burst balloon, but she soon blew herself up again. "But I've been invited to fly in it, tho there! The man told me he would take me up next time. It whirred when it flew away."

Maisie whirred, too, waving her arms about

to let Macpherson see what a helicopter looked like. She had forgiven him for going off without her. Maisie was not one to sulk for long. Now that he was back, she wanted to share everything with him. "I'll athk him to take you up, too," she said kindly.

"Huh!" said Macpherson, pretending not to be interested, but he was interested all right. He would have liked to hear every single thing about the helicopter but not with the grocer sitting glaring at him. Grandpa sensed the boy's uneasiness. He always knew what Macpherson was feeling.

"I'm turning in early," he said, stretching and yawning. "I'm too full of food and fresh air! I expect you're ready to drop anchor, too, Macpherson. Away you go up to that room of yours. Tomorrow's another day."

Old Skinflint was still there in the morning. So were Macpherson's bruises. But his spirits were back to normal. Nothing was going to spoil his holiday. He went whizzing out into the sunshine followed by the dog and the donkey, and by Maisie who was wearing her new blue dress.

"Hooray!" he shouted, for no reason at all, and took a great leap into the air. "Isn't it great?"

"Yeth, ithn't it?" agreed Maisie. "What'll we do?"

There were a hundred things they could do. They could explore the cave, fish in the loch, ride the donkey, lie on the beach, pick fruit in the garden, climb up to the flag-tower....

"*Crying cockles and mussels, alive, alive O!* Hullo, you two! Would you like to come with me?" shouted the Boy. It was the last day of his weekend on the island, and he, too, meant to make the most of it. He was dressed in an old kilt and jersey, and seemed as ready as Macpherson to jump into the air and shout hooray.

"Yes, we're coming," said Macpherson, speaking for both of them. "Where?"

"Och, just anywhere. Come on!"

"Cheerio!" called Grandpa. "Enjoy yourselves!"

He was sitting on a bench at the door with the grocer by his side. Old Skinflint's foot was resting on a stool which Mrs Thing had brought out from the kitchen. Morag McConnochie was doing her best to spoil him; but what did he care for cream on his porridge? He did not even look at the seagulls or the scenery. All he wanted was to get back to the shop to count the money in the till. Goodness knew how Miss Peacock would be getting on without him.

"She'll be getting on fine, if I know my cousin," said Mrs Thing, guessing his thoughts. ("Better than if you were there," she thought to herself.) "Just relax, Mr McGlashan, and forget all your worries. You can leave later on, when the Boy goes. He'll drive you to Glasgow, if your foot's still sore. Sit still now; I'll be bringing you out a glass of milk in a wee while."

Old Skinflint scowled after her and said, "A glass of milk, after all that breakfast! They do nothing but eat here. I never met such a wasteful family."

"They've got hearts of gold," said Grandpa mildly. "Take a look at the Ben, Mr McGlashan. Did you ever see such a sight?"

"Silly goat!" growled the grocer, but he was not talking to Grandpa. He was scolding himself for his sudden impulse to climb the mountain. "I can't think what came over me taking such a daft notion."

"It would be a dull world without daft notions," grinned the old man. "I'm glad you've still got the spirit of adventure in you, Mr McGlashan. It keeps you young."

The grocer gave a groan as he stretched out

his sore foot on the stool. All the same, he began to thaw a little in Grandpa's company. He was not exactly smiling when Mrs Thing came out carrying a tray with two glasses of milk and a plateful of scones. But at least the grim look had left his face. He even helped himself to one of the scones, spread liberally with butter and home-made strawberry jam.

"I can't understand how I'm feeling hungry. I've never eaten so much in my life," he mumbled, and took a gulp from the glass, leaving himself with a milky moustache.

"It is the good air," said Mrs Thing with a gleam of triumph in her eyes. "If I had you here for a week or two, I would be making a new man of you, Mr McGlashan."

She would, too! She had already made a new man of Grandpa. His cough was gone, he was no longer looking as thin as a skeleton, his eyes were brighter and his step brisker. Aunt Janet was going to get the surprise of her life when they arrived back at Clyde-View Tower. So was the District Nurse.

"I doubt if Joey the budgie will recognise me," chuckled the old man. "There's no place like Seagull Island for pepping you up."

But it would take more than a glass of milk and a home-baked scone to pep up Old

Skinflint. Still, he had an unusual feeling of contentment as he sat in the sun letting his thoughts wander. They wandered, of course, back to the shop, even while he was looking at the Ben. Yet in days to come the grocer would remember this brief holiday with a faint stirring of pleasure.

By now the others were at the far side of the island ready to explore the cave.

"You stay out," boomed Roderick, pushing the dog and donkey aside. "We'll have to get down on our hands and knees and crawl. Are you game, youngsters?"

"Rather!" said Macpherson eagerly. But Maisie's "Y—Yeth!" was not so assured.

She followed the others in, but soon crawled out backwards when she found how dark it was inside the cave. "*Haw-haw-haw!*" brayed Dum-Dum. If he could not go in himself, then he wanted some company outside. But the dog sat alone at the mouth of the cave, watching and waiting.

Macpherson was sure he would find some lost treasure hidden in a far corner of the cave. Spanish gold, maybe, from a sunken galleon; jewels beyond price; pearls and diamonds worth a king's ransom.

He could see it all in his imagination. He

would be richer than Miss Peacock's cousin from America. He would buy Grandpa a yacht and Aunt Janet a mink coat. Maisie could have a box of the best chocolates every day, including Sunday. And for himself he would buy a helicopter like Lord Kyle's.

Just then something bumped against his bare knee. Lost treasure? No! Even in the dim cave he could see that it was only an old tin can. Then suddenly he heard a faint sound. "Listen!" he whispered to his companion. "There's something alive in the cave!"

5

The Tomboy

"Oh, help!"

"Watch where you're going!"

Macpherson and Roderick let out cries of alarm at the same moment. They had just bumped their heads together in the darkness of the cave. It was Macpherson who suffered most, for the Boy's head was a great deal bigger and harder than his. For a second he saw stars, then he felt something fluttering against his face. It flew past him and went winging away out into the sunshine.

"Och! It's only a seagull," he said in a disappointed voice.

Roderick laughed, a great laugh which echoed round the cave. "What did you expect? A castaway? Hold on, Macpherson; here's something. A bottle! Maybe there's a message in it. No! What a shame! It's empty."

Macpherson let out a sudden yell and drew back as his hands came in contact with something sharp and prickly. "What's this? Look out, Roderick. Maybe it's dangerous."

"Oh, yes, very dangerous!" Roderick poked at the prickly object. "It's a hedgehog. Come along, Sleepy-head. Out into the sunshine."

It was easy enough for Macpherson to crawl backwards out of the cave and to take the hedgehog with him. Not so easy for Roderick. He seemed to have swelled to an even larger size since he had gone in. "Oh dear! I'm here for life," he said, in a comical voice. "Give me a tug."

Macpherson tugged with all his might, while Maisie, in turn, tugged him. The hedgehog rolled itself into a prickly ball to protect itself

from the dog, who had taken one sniff at it and then let out a startled yelp. "*Haw-haw!*" brayed Dum-Dum, but it was no laughing matter. The dog turned his back in a huff and rubbed his sore nose on the grass. The hedgehog was safe, as far as he was concerned.

"Breathe in," advised Macpherson; but Roderick only grinned and shook his head.

"I'll never make it. It's all that steak-and-kidney pudding," he groaned. But at last he managed to wriggle through the narrow opening, and he rolled out on to the grass beside the hedgehog.

For a time they all sat soaking in the sunshine and watching the seagulls taking off and landing on the rocks, like little aeroplanes. Then suddenly Macpherson sat up. He had caught sight of a small boat bobbing towards the island. Someone seemed to be waving to them.

"Look! Is that someone in trouble? They're trying to attract our attention."

"So they are!" Roderick sprang to his feet. "I don't like the look of the loch. It's like the Ben; it takes turns. One moment it's calm and the next it begins to boil."

It was true! The water, which had looked so peaceful a few moments before, had begun to heave and swirl, tossing the small boat from side to side. "It looks as if he's lost his oars," cried Macpherson, slithering down the bank to the water's edge.

"It'th not a him; it'th a her!" said Maisie, scrambling after him.

"Whoever it is, they'll be in the loch in two toots," roared Roderick. They were all down at the water's edge by now, except the hedgehog who had crawled back to the safety of the cave. "Ahoy! Do you need help?" called Roderick.

The next moment he was ready to plunge into the water. They could see the boat overturning and a figure falling into the loch. But before Roderick could rush to the rescue, the figure struck out for the shore, swimming strongly and steadily as if in a race.

They all reached out hands to help her over the rocks. "Gee! thanks," she said, shaking herself like a wet seal. "Say! This is some loch. It was as calm as a mill-pond when I set out, and look at it now."

She smiled at them in a friendly fashion,not in the least upset by her adventure. Her long blonde hair was wringing wet, but she tossed it back carelessly. She did not seem to notice that her jeans and pullover were also soaking. There was a tomboy look about her, as if she was used to such happenings.

Macpherson wondered how old she was–sixteen perhaps?–and where she came from. Her accent was American, and judging by her suntanned skin, she was used to an open-air life. He liked her carefree look. A pity, he thought, that she wasn't a boy!

"What about the boat?" asked Roderick, looking at the small craft drifting in the water. "Is it yours?"

The girl shook her head. "No, I just hired it for the day. I guess it'll drift ashore. I'll pay for any damage," she said carelessly. "I guess I'd better run about a bit and try to get dry. Are there any houses near here?"

"There's the castle," Roderick told her.

"The castle! My! This must be Seagull Island!" Her eyes were sparkling. "Say! That's great! I've arrived, even if the boat hasn't."

They looked at her in surprise. Who was she, and why had she come to visit Seagull Island? Roderick did his best to find out. "You've come from America?" he asked.

"That's right; I have. But not today." The girl laughed and shook out her damp hair. "And I'm not American. I'm Scottish to the core. Mom and Dad took me to New York when I was a baby. But now they've come back to settle in their native land. Gee! I'm so thrilled! My name's Flora, by the way. That's Scottish enough. After Flora Macdonald, you know. She was the one who helped Bonnie Prince Charlie to escape."

"Yes, I've heard of her!" said Roderick solemnly. "I'm called Roderick. After nobody in particular. It's a common enough name in Scotland. And here's Macpherson, and Miss Maisie Murphy. The donkey's called Dum-Dum, and the dog's just the dog. That's the lot! Tell me, Flora, how did you know about Seagull Island?"

"Mom and Dad told me about it. They have a cousin—or maybe she's a second-cousin—living here in the castle. Morag McConnochie!"

"Mercy me!" Macpherson stared at the girl. "Is your dad called Robert Reid?"

"That's right."

"Jings! You must be a millionaire!"

The girl threw back her head and laughed. "Gee! I wish I was." Then she looked serious for a moment. "No, I don't. I'd sooner have this lovely scenery and that little lock."

"*Loch!*" Macpherson corrected her.

"Sorry! I must get my accent right. As for being a millionaire, I don't know how you figured that out. My dad's certainly not poor. He worked hard in America and so did Mom.

I'm going to work, too, and help them to run their restaurants in Glasgow. They're back there just now—Mom and Dad—looking for a new home. But I just had to come and see Seagull Island. I've heard so much about it." She turned to Macpherson. "Say! How did you know my dad's name?"

"Well, you see," began Macpherson, starting to tell the story from the beginning; but Roderick stopped him.

"We can talk about that later. Come along, Flora; it's time you changed those wet clothes. Mum'll be delighted to see you. She's Morag McConnochie, by the way."

The girl took a little skip into the air and cried, "Isn't that something! Life sure is full of wonderful surprises. I can't wait to see a real castle."

They set off with the dog and donkey leading the way and with Maisie Murphy trailing far behind. Her chubby face was usually wreathed in smiles; but now her lip was pouting and she seemed on the verge of tears.

"What's up with you?" asked Macpherson, turning to look at her.

"N-Nothing," gulped Maisie, wiping away a tear with the back of her hand. But Macpherson knew it was not "nothing". She was feeling left out because another lassie was taking up his attention. Girls! They were hopeless!

"Come on, softie!" he said, grasping her by the hand.

Maisie looked up at him through her tears. "Flora'th a lovely name, ithn't it?" she sighed, and gave him a sidelong glance.

"Away!" said Macpherson stoutly. "It's not half as nice as Maisie."

Maisie beamed. It was like the sun coming out from behind a dark cloud. She could put up with Flora as long as Macpherson didn't think too much of her.

Grandpa and Old Skinflint were still sitting on the bench in the sunshine. The old man was smoking his pipe, but the grocer did not indulge in such wasteful habits. His eyes were half closed and he was totting up sums of money in his mind. If only he had brought the shop-ledger with him, he could have done some useful homework.

He opened his eyes when he saw the little group come trooping towards the castle. "Silly goats!" he grunted, losing the answer to the sum in his head. "What are they up to now? Youngsters! They're nothing but idiots. And who's that girl with them, all dripping wet?"

"We'll soon find out," said Grandpa. "She

looks like a mermaid just out of the sea. Ahoy, Macpherson! What's the news?"

There was so much to tell, Macpherson did not know where to begin. Luckily, Mrs Thing came out at that moment and took one look at the girl. Without asking needless questions, she hustled her inside. "Dry clothes! That's what you need," she said briskly. Explanations could come later.

"Her name'th Flora," said Maisie, sitting down at Grandpa's feet.

"Flora, eh? That's a nice name," said Grandpa unwisely.

"Oh, do you think tho?"

"Of course, Maisie's better," said the old man hastily. "Where did you find her? In the loch?"

They all began to talk at once. The story had no beginning, middle, or end; but Grandpa got the hang of it all right. So did Old Skinflint. Especially after Macpherson fixed him with a gaze and told him the best titbit of all. "Mr McGlashan, sir," he said in an important voice. "D'you know what?"

The grocer's eyebrows began to quiver. "That's a stupid thing to say. What do you mean by it?" he asked.

Macpherson took a deep breath and scored a

bull's-eye. "You remember Miss Peacock's rich cousin from America? Robert Reid. Well, Flora's his daughter."

The grocer's eyebrows began to twitch, and he cried, "Miss Flora Reid! Well, isn't that lucky? Her father's coming to see me in the shop next week. I'm hoping to do business with him." He rubbed his hands together. "I'll be delighted to meet his daughter and do anything I can to help her. Delighted!"

Macpherson had never seen Old Skinflint delighted before, or even faintly pleased. But was it delight or greed that shone in the grocer's eyes? The sun, the scenery, Grandpa's words of wisdom, all were lost on him. Never mind the beauty of the Ben. The prospect of making more money was far more attractive.

Flora came out of the castle with her long hair tied back with a ribbon. She was wearing an old tartan skirt and a red jersey. "Aunt Morag's," she said, laughing at herself. "It's hardly the right size, but who cares? I say, isn't she a darling? And Uncle Archie, too!"

Uncle Archie! It was difficult for Macpherson to think of Mr Thing as Archie. But the main thing was that Flora was delighted with her new relatives, and thrilled at the thought of living in a castle. "They've asked me to stay, but I'll have to get word back to Mom and Dad in Glasgow."

This was Old Skinflint's chance. "May I offer my services, Miss Flora?" he said, in the voice he kept for his best customers. He held out his hand. "McGlashan, the grocer; established 1900! I'll be going back to Glasgow tonight, and can contact your parents for you. As a matter of fact, I've already been in touch with your father. I'm hoping he'll become one of my customers; and you, of course, will always be welcome in my shop. Very welcome indeed!"

"Is that the shop where Macpherson works? Oh, well, I'll be coming to see him, no doubt. Thanks, Mr McGlashan," she said in a cool voice. Macpherson had a feeling that she had already made up her mind about the grocer. Flora was no fool! He was sure of this when he saw how she and Grandpa took to each other. His heart warmed towards her when she turned to him and said, "Say! Aren't you lucky, Macpherson? I think your Grandpa's a great guy." Flora was okay!

But she was not one to stand still for long. In spite of her ducking, she wanted to explore every inch of the island and was ready for any adventure. "As good as a boy," thought

Macpherson. They had climbed trees, ridden the donkey, explored the dungeons of the castle, and built a sandy skyscraper on the beach. Maisie was left behind, until the Boy took her in hand.

"Oh dear! I can't keep up with those two," he said, pretending to be out of breath. "D'you know what I'd like to do? Swing!"

"Thwing? Where?"

"On a swing, of course. There's one in the wood. I used to play on it when I was young. Let's go and see if it's still there."

"Oh yeth; let'th!"

Maisie put her small hand in his and trotted off at his side, forgetting her jealousy for the moment. The swing was still quite safe. After testing it, Roderick hoisted Maisie on to the seat and let her sway about to get the feel of it.

"Thith ith great!" she cried, urging him to push her higher.

"Hold tight!" boomed Roderick, giving her a mighty push. "*Ha-ha-ha! You and me . . .*"

He continued to sing and swing, while Maisie screamed with delight. "Oh! I can thee right over the tree-topth. I'm nearly ath high ath the Ben." There was a look of complete bliss on her face, and she could have swung backwards and forwards all day long.

She was one up on Macpherson now. He had never flown higher than the tree-tops. He had not felt the breathtaking thrill of swishing through the air like the man on the flying trapeze. He did not know what the castle tower looked like from the air. Roderick gave her another powerful heave which sent her up-up-up almost into the battlements.

Suddenly the swing wobbled and Maisie let out a frightened scream.

"What's up?" cried Roderick, waiting to catch her as she swung down.

"There! Up on the tower," she cried in a trembling voice. "It'th a thpook!"

"Now, now!" soothed Roderick. "Spooks don't appear in broad daylight. They don't apear at all. . . . My goodness, you're right!"

His voice trailed off, and his face suddenly seemed a shade paler. He was not one to believe in ghosts. Yet, there it was before his eyes—a white-clad figure gliding about on the battlements.

6

Comings And Goings

The ding-dong of the dinner-bell was heard, rung by Mr Thing at the door of the castle. "Food!" he shouted. "Come and get it!"

The ghostly figure up near the tower let out a shriek of laughter and vanished from sight. Roderick's face was still pale, but now that the "thpook" had gone, he had to pretend he had never seen it. Maisie, too, was willing to forget it, if she could keep on swinging.

"More! Thwing me again!" she called out, but Roderick firmly lifted her down and strode off into the castle. The first person he met face-to-face was the ghost itself, gliding downstairs trailing a long white sheet behind it.

It was Flora! "Couldn't resist it!" she said, her eyes sparkling with mischief. "I went up to change into my dry clothes, and whipped a sheet off the bed. I hope I didn't alarm you. It was just for fun."

Roderick said nothing but Maisie gave the ghost a cool look and said, "I think you're thilly." Then she turned her back and stumped off into the kitchen.

"Well!" said Flora, "that's put me in my place. I guess I deserved it. Mom and Dad are always telling me I should think before I act, but I'm not made that way." She sighed, folded up the sheet, and tried her best to look prim and proper.

At the table she made another attempt to get back into Maisie's good graces, but with little success.

"Did you enjoy your swing, little girl?" she asked in a sweet voice.

"Yeth, thank you; but I'm not a little girl," said Maisie coldly. "*I'm* thenthible."

"Oh!" Flora sat back, defeated. But she had no trouble in finding a friendly companion on the other side. Old Skinflint was only too ready to pass plates and press food on her, as if *he* had provided it instead of Mrs Thing.

"More potatoes, Miss Flora? Another helping of gravy? You must be hungry after your ducking."

"Oh, that was nothing," said Flora in an airy voice. "Nothing to the adventures I had in America. Especially when I stayed on a ranch and rode with the cowboys."

Macpherson listened eagerly to every word, but Maisie turned a deaf ear and gave all her attention to the food. This was the Boy's last meal on the island, and his mother was determined to see that he ate his fill. She piled more and more food on his plate, and in between Flora's chatter urged him, "Eat up, Boy! It'll be a long time before you see a square meal again."

Roderick reminded her that he did sometimes eat during the week and that he would be back home again next weekend. "I'm not going on a hunger strike, you know, Mum, though maybe it would do my tum a lot of good." But nothing would convince Mrs Thing that the Boy did not starve when he was out of her sight.

They had reached the pudding stage—second helpings—when the telephone rang somewhere in a back room. Macpherson scarcely heard it. He was too absorbed in Flora's stirring story of how she rode a bucking bronco while rounding up the cattle.

"It's for you, Flora," Mr Thing came back and told her. "Your dad's on the line. He managed to trace you here."

"Right," said Flora, jumping up. "I'll tell you the rest of the story when I come back, Macpherson." But when she returned she had other things on her mind. "Say, folks, d'you know what? Mom and Dad want me to go back to Glasgow tonight. They've found a house and they want me to have a look at it before they make up their minds to buy it. It's called *The Towers*. Isn't that something? I can't wait to see it. I guess I can come back to the island some other time."

It was like Flora to jump from one thing to another. For the moment she could talk about nothing but her new home. "I hope there's a big garden and room to keep a pony. You must come and visit me, Macpherson. You, too, little girl," she added, turning to Maisie.

"No, thankth!" said Maisie, with her mouth full of pudding. "I live in a Tower already. Clyde-View Tower."

"You mean the skyscraper! Oh, but this is a real house in its own grounds." Flora looked at Old Skinflint. "Did you say you were driving back to Glasgow, Mr McGlashan?"

Old Skinflint nearly swallowed his spoon in his eagerness to say, "Yes! I'd be delighted to give you a lift, Miss Flora. Delighted!"

"What about your ankle?" asked Mrs Thing. "Don't you think you ought to stay a bit longer and give it a chance to heal?"

"No, no," said the grocer impatiently. "It's much better. I've wasted enough time already.

I must get back to business." The very word business brought a glint to his eyes. He could see Flora's rich father coming into the shop and saying gratefully, "You've been very kind to my daughter, Mr McGlashan. I'll be giving you a big order each week." Even Old Skinflint could have his dreams, though they were very down-to-earth ones.

Mrs Thing's eyes were full of tears at the thought of parting from the Boy. She loaded him with butter, cakes, and scones—"A wee bite to see you through the week"—and stood at the shore waving till the boat was out of sight. "Oh deary me," she sighed, turning back to the empty castle. "It will be many a long day before I set eyes on him again."

"He's coming back next weekend," Macpherson reminded her. "That's not long."

"It's long enough. Och well, what about a wee cup of tea?" she said, cheering up at the prospect.

"No, thanks. I'm too full," said Macpherson; but Grandpa had enough sense to say, "Tea? Just what I need. Come along, Mrs Thing; let's put the kettle on, and drown our sorrows!"

The island seemed deserted except for the seagulls circling overhead. There were always a dozen or more waltzing about in the sky, as if keeping an eye on their own property. "This is our island, don't forget it. Seagull Island! Seagull! Seagull!" they seemed to be screaming.

Macpherson kicked his heels. He was glad Old Skinflint had gone. How could he enjoy his holiday with the grocer's beady eyes fixed on him? But he was sorry the Boy had left, and Flora, too.

"Macpherthon!" called Maisie, delighted to have her hero to herself again. "If you like, I'll let you on the thwing."

It was a great sacrifice, for she would have liked nothing better than to get on the swing herself. But anything to please Macpherson. She swung him to and fro, trying with all her might to push harder so that he, too, might see over the tree-tops. "Keep it up, Maisie. Faster!" he called in his lordly way. "Jings! It's a great feeling! I'll let you on later, if you're good!"

Soon after breakfast the next morning the helicopter came back. It hovered over the island and then dropped down to land on the grass at the far side of the castle.

Macpherson and Grandpa had been having

a heart-to-heart talk. The old man was sitting on the bench at the door with the boy sprawling at his feet. So much had happened lately that Macpherson had missed his usual talks with Grandpa. But now they were alone, except for the dog and Dum-Dum, and they were making the most of it. It was like picking up the dropped stitches in a piece of knitting. Neither of them stopped till every stitch had been sorted out.

"That's us ship-shape again, Macpherson my boy," said the old man, puffing at his pipe. "It's fine to be on our own for a change."

Even Maisie was out of the way for once. Miss Murphy had taken it into her head to learn how to cook. Mrs Thing could turn out tasty meals in next to no time. Perhaps Maisie could find out how to do the same for the Murphies. Fish-and-chips from a paper bag was *their* greatest treat. But the family rarely had real sit-down meals, with second helpings for everybody.

"Can I begin with baking, Mithith Thing?" Maisie asked her hostess, who was only too pleased to have such a willing pupil.

"Certainly, my dear," said Mrs Thing, tying a large white apron round Maisie's waist. "Let's start with something simple: scones.

Then I'll show you how to bake a gingerbread."

Maisie's cheeks were scarlet and she was up to the elbows in flour when she heard the whirring sound in the sky.

"It'th the helicopter," she cried, dashing to the door and leaving a white trail behind her.

"Come back," said Mrs Thing firmly. "You'll never become a cook if you leave things half done. Finish making the scones and Lord Kyle can have one with his cup of tea. I'll put the kettle on and we'll just have it in the kitchen. He's an ordinary man, in spite of being a lord."

Macpherson was agog with excitement when the helicopter landed, and could hardly wait to see who would come out. "Mercy me! Is that him!" he cried, when a small man, wearing a check suit with baggy plus-fours, set foot on the ground. "He looks like a—a ..." He could find no words to describe the man.

"A wee Scots comic!" chuckled Grandpa, who had met Lord Kyle on his previous visit. "He sounds like one, too! Ship ahoy, Lord Kyle! Welcome back."

The little man kicked up his heels and did a few funny dance-steps on the grass while Dum-Dum looked on and brayed, *"Haw-haw-haw!"*

"Who d'you think you're laughing at, you daft donkey!" cried Lord Kyle, thumping the animal on the back. Then he made his way towards Grandpa, calling, "I've dropped doon from the skies to give you a wee surprise. Is this the fella you were talking aboot? Macpherson's the name?"

"Yes, sir; Lord Kyle, sir," said Macpherson, standing to attention.

"Hoots-toots! Less of the sirs and lords," grinned the small man, squatting down on the grass like a little gnome. "I'm just plain Jock Scott, the same as I was before her Majesty gave me a fancy title. Jock Scott, the builder."

"You mean, you build houses?" asked Macpherson.

"Sure! Hooses galore, all shapes and sizes."

"Not only houses," broke in Grandpa. "He builds skyscrapers, too. Guess what, Macpherson."

"He built Clyde-View Tower!"

"The very same," said the little man, grinning up at them. "It's a good strong building, though I say it myself. A Jock Scott building! Though, mind you, nothing as strong as this one here." He took an admiring look at the crumbling old castle. "It's a bit of a ruin now, right enough; but don't forget it's stood up for many hundreds of years. Man! I wish I could have met the builder. He must have been a great chap, yon!"

He sat there musing about the past till Mrs Thing appeared at the door, calling, "Do you fancy a cup of tea, m'Lord?"

"Hoots-toots! Why else d'you think I flew here, Mrs McConnochie. Lead me to it."

Maisie was waiting for them in the kitchen, ready to pass round a plateful of newly-baked scones. "They're ever tho good. I made them mythelf," she said, with her usual lack of modesty. All the same, there was an anxious look on her face as she watched Lord Kyle take his first bite.

"The best I've ever tasted. Even better than Mrs McConnochie's, and that's saying a lot." He winked at Mrs Thing and helped himself to another scone even before he had finished the first. "I think the baker deserves a reward. What aboot a ride in the helicopter, my wee lassie?"

"Oh, yeth, pleathe!" She began to take her apron off, there and then. "Macpherson, too?"

"Sure! The more the merrier!"

Macpherson gave Maisie a thumb's-up signal. There was one thing about her, she wasn't selfish. A ride in a helicopter! "Jings! Am I not lucky?" he burst out.

"What about my gingerbread?" asked Maisie, with a worried look at the oven. "Could you keep an eye on it, Mithith Thing?"

"Both eyes, my dear! Off you go and forget it."

Grandpa waved them off. "*Ho-ro! up she rises!* Cheerio, Macpherson. Watch out for the man in the moon."

"Merthy! Are we going ath high ath that?" said Maisie, looking alarmed; but Macpherson hustled her on board and said, "Don't be daft; it's just a joke."

The little man had now taken on a different role. He was no longer Lord Kyle. Or even Jock Scott, the builder. He was a pilot. He sat apart from them, and gave all his attention to the job in hand. Mr Thing acted as his assistant on the ground, and soon Macpherson and Maisie heard the helicopter begin to whirr and throb.

"Can I hold your hand, Macpherthon?"

"If you like."

The truth was, the boy was glad to have something to clutch, even if it was only Maisie's sticky little paw. It was a strange feeling, taking off, like going up suddenly in a lift. It took their breath away.

The castle seemed to have toppled sideways.

Even Grandpa looked upside-down and the loch was hanging from the sky. Then suddenly the helicopter gave a little shudder and straightened itself. It was okay! Things were back in their right places, and they were soaring away up to the top of the Ben.

7

Air Adventures

"This is easier than climbing the Ben," thought the boy, as he soared over the snow-topped mountain. "Oh my! We're away up to the clouds."

Macpherson and Maisie seemed to be all alone in the sky, flying even higher than the birds. Maisie's eyes were wide with surprise and she gasped out, "Are we really going to the moon, Macpherthon?"

"Of course not. The moon's much too far away," he said in a superior voice. He was growing used to being airborne. "Look! We're away above the Ben."

It was only a small hill by now, hardly a mountain at all. As for Seagull Island, it had vanished from sight. Now they were whirring away over unknown lochs and bens.

"Macpherthon, I can thee houtheth!"

"Away!" said Macpherson; but Maisie was right. He could see not only houses—but skyscrapers as well.

"We're over Glasgow! Look, Maisie; there's

the River Clyde."

"Tho it ith. D'you think we'll thee Clyde-View Tower?"

They had a faint homesick feeling, flying over their own town. The helicopter hovered lower and lower. Jock Scott the builder was taking a look at some of his own work! Macpherson and Maisie strained their eyes to see if they could recognise anybody. Aunt Janet, maybe, shaking a duster out of the window. But no! They could only see toy cars and vans scurrying along the streets like little mice.

The helicopter made its way upwards and changed course. Where were they off to now? They were flying over the sea! Surely Lord Kyle was not going to take them as far as America!

"It's only the Firth of Clyde," Macpherson told himself. The great ships were there, sailing off to far countries where Grandpa himself had sailed in his younger days. How small they looked from the sky, as small as the model ships Grandpa now made.

Now they had turned round and were on their homeward flight towards the island and the Ben. But where was the mountain? Lost in the mist! It was the same white woolly fog through which Macpherson and Roderick had battled on their way down the Ben. No pilot could find his way through such a maze.

"Are we lotht?" asked Maisie, gazing out of the window and seeing nothing. She was not really alarmed, not with Macpherson sitting by her side.

The boy shook his head. He did not know whether they were lost or not. But he could feel the helicopter circling round as if Lord Kyle was looking for a gap in the mist; and soon he found it, and they were out into the sunshine once more.

"Are we away back to Glathgow?" asked Maisie, as the familiar skyscrapers came into view again. "What'th wrong?"

"Don't know," admitted Macpherson. "I suppose he can't land on Seagull Island until the mist lifts. Perhaps he's just going to fly around. Or maybe he's going to land somewhere else."

Somewhere else was the answer! The helicopter flew over the skyscrapers, over the river, and then hovered above a house somewhere in the outskirts of the city. It was a large house, with a tower almost as high as the castle's. There was a green lawn in front of the house. "That's where we're going to land," cried

Macpherson, leaning over to look.

They were flying sideways now, ready for landing. Steady does it! Macpherson held his breath. "Watch it, Lord Kyle!" But Jock Scott the builder knew what he was doing, whether he was directing a bulldozer or a helicopter.

"Spot on!" cried the boy as they landed dead-centre on the lawn. He peered out of the window, wondering whose house this was, and if Lord Kyle would let them stretch their legs and explore.

"Look! There'th Mith Peacock," cried Maisie, waving wildly to a figure making her way towards them across the lawn.

"Rubbish!" scoffed Macpherson. "What would Miss Peacock be doing in a place like this? Good gracious . . .!"

Miss Peacock was smiling and waving to him. She was wearing her "good" dress and looked younger and happier away from Mr McGlashan's shop. But what on earth was she doing here, shaking hands with Lord Kyle? The little man had jumped down from the cockpit and strutted across the grass to meet her.

Before Macpherson could recover from his surprise, another was in store for him. A girl came running out of the house, tossing her long fair hair over her shoulder. She turned a cartwheel on the lawn and landed, laughing, beside Miss Peacock and Lord Kyle.

"It's Flora!" cried Macpherson, eager to get out and join her. "Look, Maisie!"

"I can thee," said Maisie in a cold voice. "When ith the man going to fly uth home?"

But the man was not going back yet. "Tumble oot, kids!" he called, opening the door for them. "We're stuck here till the mist clears. How do you like *The Towers*? One of my hooses. A Jock Scott building. I've been living here myself, but now I'm selling it to this lassie's father."

Of course! Robert Reid From America! Miss Peacock's rich cousin! Flora's father! Macpherson added it all up and sorted it out in his head, like one of Old Skinflint's sums.

Miss Peacock was smiling and nodding at him. "Fancy you dropping down from the sky, Macpherson! I came here with Flora to look at the new house, and here you are!"

"Yes, here I am, Miss Peacock. How's Old Skinflint?"

"Him!" She made a little face. "His ankle's improving, but not his temper. Make the most of your holiday, Macpherson."

"Oh yes, I will, Miss Peacock; and it's all

thanks to you. You're a gem!"

"Tuts!" It was not easy to pay compliments to Miss Peacock. She turned to Flora and said, "You've met, you two, haven't you?"

"Yes, on the island," said Macpherson. "Hullo, Flora; how do you like your new house?"

"Gee! It's swell; and it's swell to see you again, Macpherson. You, too, little girl," said Flora, turning to Maisie who had sat down on the grass and was busy making herself a daisy-chain. "How are you?"

"Fine, thankth." That was the end of the conversation, as far as Maisie was concerned; but nothing could stop Flora's chattering tongue. She thrust her arm through Macpherson's and said, "Come and see over the house. And the stables, too. Did I tell you Dad's going to buy me a pony? I'd sure like to do some show-jumping. Maybe I'll win one of those silver cups."

There was no maybe about it. She would! If Miss Flora Reid made up her mind about anything, it was as good as done. Maisie watched them go and bit her lip to keep it from trembling. She hung the daisy-chain round her neck and looked up at Miss Peacock.

"Can Flora bake?" she asked her.

"Oh, I hardly think so."

"Well, I can!" said Maisie, with a note of triumph in her voice. "Tho there!"

Miss Peacock smiled. "Good for you, Maisie. You're one up."

"Yeth, I am," said Maisie smugly.

They flew back when the mist had cleared, over the Ben, over the loch, and at last over the little island. Grandpa was there, watching and waving. It was a fine feeling to be coming home again.

"I hope my gingerbread'th all right," said Maisie, trotting away into the castle kitchen. She could take adventures in her stride, but it was the homely things she liked best.

Lord Kyle sampled the gingerbread before he flew away again. "Ay, you're a grand baker, my wee lassie," he said, smacking his lips. "Weel, I'm away! Maybe I'll look in to see you in Clyde-View Tower, when you get back to Glasgow. Tooral-oo!"

It was coming nearer—the day when they must return to Glasgow. Macpherson tried to push the thought to the back of his mind. He filled every single second of every day, and was delighted to see how Grandpa, too, was making the most of his holiday.

"*Oh, I do like to be beside the seaside!*" sang the old man in a chuckly voice. They were wading up to their knees in the water near the sandy beach. Grandpa had rolled up his trousers and was skipping about like a youngster. "I wonder what your Aunt Janet would say if she could see me now?"

"She would say you should have more sense at your age! But I'm glad you haven't, Grandpa," said Macpherson, looking fondly at the old man.

At that moment they heard a loud *toot-toot* from a steamer. The seagulls went winging away to meet it, screaming, "Seagull Island! Seagull! Seagull! Keep away!" But the boat was making straight for the jetty.

"I hope to goodness it's not going to land here," said Macpherson, with a scowl on his face. Like the seagulls, he did not want the peace of his island disturbed. "What a cheek they have!"

A band was playing on board and the boat seemed overloaded with children all shouting and screaming. They hung over the side, waving balloons and banners, making such a din that even the seagulls were silenced.

Maisie came running to the shore, crying, "What'th up?" She had been on the swing, swaying blissfully to and fro and singing, "*Three blind mithe; thee how they run....*"

Mr and Mrs Thing also came hurrying to the landing-stage. "It's a school picnic," said Mr Thing, giving them a wave of welcome. "Lord Kyle lets them come and hold it here on the island. It's a tricky job getting a boat that size alongside our small pier. Come on, lend a hand, Macpherson."

Macpherson came, but he was grumbling away inside himself. "A school picnic! They'll be running races and making ever such a noise and ever such a mess. It's not fair! Spoiling our nice island."

Grandpa, the wise old bird, had guessed his thoughts. He rolled down his trouser legs and said, "Good luck to them! You wouldn't grudge them one afternoon here, would you, Macpherson? We've had nearly two weeks."

Grandpa was right, of course. All the same, Macpherson still thought the newcomers were nuisances. Especially when they came swarming on shore and began doing everything at once. Chasing the donkey; taking possession of the swing; throwing stones into the water and frightening the swans; shinning up trees; teasing the dog; whooping and shouting like animals let loose from the zoo.

There was noise and confusion on all sides. The teachers made an effort to keep their brood under control, then gave it up and sat in a little group by themselves on the shore. Let the children do what they liked! It was the teachers' day off as well, and they meant to get something out of it..

Macpherson stood and watched the revellers from a distance. But Maisie, who was a joiner-in, soon made friends with all and sundry. She was ready to run races, play hide-and seek, or just talk to anyone who would listen.

"I can cook! I've made a gingerbread and a napple-dumpling. And I've been up in a helicopter. My name'th Maithie. What'th yourth?"

There was one boy—Geordie—bigger than the rest, who took a delight in tripping the girls up, and trying to push them into the water. Macpherson kept a wary eye on him. The girls could look after themselves. But when Dum-Dum let out a cry—"*Haw-haw!*"—which sounded like a call for help, Macpherson sprang into action. The boy was pulling the donkey's ears and twisting his tail, just for the fun of tormenting him.

"Stop it, you!"

The boy swung round and took Macpherson's

measure.

"Away and chase yourself!" he said, in a voice full of contempt for one so much smaller than himself.

"I'll chase *you*, if you don't look out," warned Macpherson.

"Look who's talking!" The boy gave Macpherson a push which sent him sprawling at the donkey's feet. "Silly wee thing! Away and play with the lassies!"

Macpherson was up in a flash, his fists ready for fighting. But Grandpa suddenly appeared between them, pretending not to have noticed what was going on.

"You're the very chap I want," he said, taking Geordie by the arm. "You and Macpherson here. I need a couple of sensible young men to organise the races."

The two boys were still scowling at each other like angry fighting-cocks. Macpherson knew fine what Grandpa was up to. The old man was always one for keeping the peace; but Macpherson was not going to give in so easily, even to please Grandpa.

He turned away and said sulkily, "Let the teachers do it."

Grandpa said mildly, "Och, they're having a rest, so I offered to help. We'll need a

winning-tape, and some old sacks for the sack-race, and we'll have to start pegging out the ground. . . ."

It was no use. Macpherson had to give in. He could not risk letting Grandpa overtire himself. He gave him a half-smile, as much as to say, "You're a crafty old thing! You can't fool me!" But he did not smile at Geordie. "You wait!" he thought, as he ran off to look for empty sacks. "I'll get even with you yet."

The strange thing was that once the races started he began to enjoy himself. After all, he had wanted a companion of his own age on the island. Now he had plenty to choose from, and they were not all bullies like big Geordie. The best thing to do was ignore him.

He and Grandpa held the tape for the infants' races. They were not quite infants—that was the name the teachers gave them—but none of them could run very well. They kept stopping halfway to see if anyone else was coming.

"Ahoy! Come on! You're not into harbour yet," Grandpa called to them. More often than not, it was Dum-Dum or the dog who won.

Mr and Mrs Thing provided the prizes. They were very simple: a rosy apple, a bagful of home-made toffee, a bunch of roses, some strawberries from the castle garden, a ride on Dum-Dum for the winner.

Macpherson found himself whooping and shouting with the rest when it came to the egg-and-spoon race, the obstacle race, the three-legged race, and the sack-race. He took part in some of them himself, not winning, but enjoying all the fun, and forgetting to bother about Geordie.

That is, until the last race! That was when the bigger boys all stood in a line ready to set off for the fastest race of all. The teachers had joined them by now, refreshed after their rest and ready to cheer on the favourite—Big Geordie.

Macpherson had not meant to compete. Let Geordie get on with it and win the race. Who cared? But Grandpa said, "Here's your chance, Macpherson. I'd join in myself, if my legs weren't so shaky. Go on; I'm backing you, my boy."

He gave Macpherson a wink to show that he was taking sides, in spite of all his pretence. He wanted the boy to win. "Okay, Grandpa, I'll do my best," said Macpherson, taking up the challenge.

One-two-three-GO! They were off like a shot from a gun. It was a short sharp race.

Geordie and Macpherson were quickest off their marks, and ran neck-and-neck. The others were left, puffing, far behind. Macpherson could see Grandpa at the tape calling, "Come on, Macpherson! Come on!" He could do it. One more spurt and he would win.

He was shooting past Geordie when he tripped and fell flat on his face. But what made him trip? Was it Geordie who kicked out at him as he pushed past and sped on to the winning-tape? Macpherson was sure of it, as he picked himself up and came in last.

"Well done, Geordie! Hooray for you!" the teachers were shouting, as Mr Thing presented him with his prize, an old knife which had once belonged to the Boy.

Grandpa did not join in the applause. He gave Macpherson a look and said, "Never heed, Macpherson. It's better to run a straight race than to win."

8

Next Stop Glasgow

The steamer was toot-tooting at the pier, ready to leave. The birds circled overhead, screaming.

When it came to the parting, Macpherson felt sorry to see the strangers go. It had been fun to race and shout and fight with them. The sleepy little island had come to life. It would be very quiet when they had all gone.

He stood at the little pier with Maisie who was waving goodbye to her new friends.

"Ta-ta! I'll thee you in Glathgow."

The teachers were sorting out their brood, counting them like sheep. They were all there, except one—Big Geordie!

"Who cares?" thought Macpherson; but in the end he was forced to join in the search. The teachers were both angry and anxious. The steamer tooted, Mr Thing rang the dinner-bell, and everybody shouted; but still there was no sign of the missing boy.

Where could he be? Macpherson ran through the little wood to see if he was stuck up a tree. No! Not a sign of him. Had he fallen into the water, or tumbled over a cliff?

Suddenly he caught sight of Dum-Dum and the dog, standing at the mouth of the cave. The donkey seemed to be laughing his head off. "*Haw-haw-haw!*" But the dog was growling angrily, and barking at someone inside. It was Geordie!

"What on earth are you doing in there?" cried Macpherson. "Come out! They're all looking for you."

Big Geordie began to blubber. How like a bully to start crying the moment he was in trouble! Macpherson looked at him in disgust. "What's up?" he asked sharply.

"I can't get out. The dog won't let me. He'll bite." Big Geordie crouched back into the cave as the dog took a lunge forward, baring his teeth as if he did, indeed, mean to bite the boy.

Macpherson was puzzled. The plain dog, usually so docile, was bristling with rage.

"Here! What have you been doing to him?" he asked Geordie in a suspicious voice. "Were you tormenting him?"

"N-No! Not specially."

"What d'you mean by that? Did you hit him?" asked Macpherson angrily.

"Well—sort of! I threw some stones at him,"

admitted Geordie, still keeping a wary eye on the dog. "It was just for fun. He chased me, and I crawled in here to get out of his way. And now I can't get out." He began to blubber again, like a baby.

Macpherson was seething with rage. He could see it all. Big Geordie throwing stones at the dog "just for fun". The dog trying to dodge out of the way; then, goaded into fury, turning and chasing his tormentor.

It was all very well hurting the dog; but when it came to Geordie being hurt, there was no fun in it! Macpherson could imagine him quaking with terror as he ran for his life,

looking for a hiding-place. He had found it in the cave, but now his shelter had become his prison. The dog was waiting for him to come out, so that he could have his revenge.

Serve him right! Macpherson wanted to have *his* revenge, too. He had a good mind to go away and leave Geordie to his fate. But, of course, he couldn't. He heard another loud hoot from the steamer, and cried, "Come out, you big softie! I'll keep the dog away. Come on, dog! Good boy! It's all right; he's not worth bothering about."

Macpherson patted the dog's rough coat and spoke soothingly to him, while Geordie crept cautiously out and wiped away his cowardly tears.

"You—you'll not let on? To the others, I mean," he asked, when they were on their way to the pier. Now that the danger was past, Geordie wanted to be the big man again.

"No, I'll not let on," agreed Macpherson, giving him a look of contempt.

"Here! You can have this." Geordie brought out from his pocket the knife he had won in the race. "Take it."

"No, thanks," said Macpherson, turning away.

"Okay!" Geordie put the knife back in his

pocket and ran off to join the others. By the time he went up the gangway, he had regained his swagger.

"Where in the world have you been?" asked an anxious teacher. "We thought we'd lost you."

Big Geordie gave a cheeky grin and said, "I'm not so easily lost! I was—er—away up a tree. Ever such a high one. Right at the very top. I forgot about the time; but I'm here now, so all's well."

"All's well," said Grandpa, as the boat slid away from the jetty. He gave Macpherson a questioning look.

"Yes, everything's ship-shape, Grandpa."

The old man knew there was something to tell, but for once Macpherson was not going to say anything. He had given his word. Big Geordie gave him an impudent wave from the deck, but Macpherson did not wave back. He just looked past him.

It was raining on their last day. "Maybe it's just as well," said Grandpa, buttoning up his mackintosh. "It'll not be so difficult to say goodbye to Seagull Island."

But it was difficult enough. The island looked fresher and greener after a shower. The colours of the loch and of the Ben were more beautiful, all delicate shades of pale blues and greens and purples. The castle itself seemed more like a fortress with the rain dripping from its towers.

Maisie, too, was dripping tears as she said goodbye to Dum-Dum. She threw her arms round his wet neck and said, "Ta-ta, you! Be good!"

"*Haw!*" Dum-Dum showed his teeth, but there seemed to be tears in his eyes, too. The dog licked her bare legs, and jumped into the little boat where Mr Thing was waiting to take them across the loch.

Herself came down to see them off, with an umbrella held over her head and a large basket in her hand. Food! There were eggs and butter and honey and jam, as well as tarts and cakes and scones. "A wee reminder of the island," she said, wiping away the rain from her face.

As if they needed any reminder! They waved to her all the way across the loch till she and her umbrella faded from view. The Boy would be waiting at the other side, to drive them back to Glasgow.

The seagulls' call seemed more mournful now. "Seagull Island! Seagull! Seagull! Come

back!"

Of course, they would come back. But meantime they must look forward.

"Joey the budgie'll be glad to see us, Grandpa. And Aunt Janet, too, of course," said Macpherson, sitting close by the old man. He put the thought of Old Skinflint out of his mind. "There's always something going on in Glasgow."

"Sure, Macpherson," said Grandpa stoutly. "There's always something, if you look in the right direction."

If you have enjoyed this book, here are some others that you might like to read, also published by Knight Books:

MACPHERSON'S SKYSCRAPER

LAVINIA DERWENT

Life is never dull for Macpherson, the young errand boy, but he could never have guessed at the surprises that were in store for him that morning as he hurried to work at McGlashan's grocery shop! His first surprise was the sight of the shop – ransacked by burglars – but then came a far greater shock: the news that his home was to be pulled down . . .

KNIGHT BOOKS

MACPHERSON'S LIGHTHOUSE ADVENTURE

LAVINIA DERWENT

Things are always happening to Macpherson, the young errand boy who lives in the city with his old seadog of a grandfather and his crochety Aunt Janet. Now they're all off to the seaside for a fortnight's free holiday – and of course, there are plenty of adventures in store there for Macpherson.

There's the time Macpherson and Grandpa almost capsize in their oary-boat, thanks to the reckless Lord Roland, and when Macpherson joins the lifeboat crew to rescue a wrecked fishing boat. But most exciting of all is his adventure at the lighthouse . . . It's certainly an eventful holiday for Macpherson!

KNIGHT BOOKS

ME!

GYLES BRANDRETH

ME! is a book all about YOU!

It asks you hundreds of questions about yourself and provides you with spaces to fill in the answers. Once you have completed the book it will be a unique guide to everything there is to know about you.

There has never been a book quite like this one before!

KNIGHT BOOKS